# USBORNE CASTLE TALES
# THE ROYAL BROOMSTICK

## Heather Amery
## Illustrated by Stephen Cartwright

Language consultant: Betty Root
Series editor: Jenny Tyler

There is a little yellow duck to find on every page.

# This is Grey Stone Castle.

This is King Leo and Queen Rose. They have two children called Prince Max and Princess Alice.

Today it is raining.

"What shall we do?" says Max. "Let's go up to
see Queen Gran in her tower," says Alice.

Max and Alice climb the stairs to the tower.

The room is empty. "Where's Queen Gran?"
asks Alice. "She must have gone out," says Max.

"There's a broomstick."

"Let's pretend it's a horse," says Alice. "Queen
Gran says we mustn't touch anything," says Max.

Alice gets on the broomstick.

"Look, Max, it's moving. Quick, get on," says Alice. The broomstick flies around the room.

"What shall we do?"

"Hold on tight," says Max. They fly out of the
window and around the top of the tower.

"Where are we going?"

"How do you steer a broomstick?" asks Max.
"I don't know but I'm not scared," says Alice.

The broomstick flies on.

It flies near a very tall tree. "Look!" says Max.
"I can see something moving in the tree."

"It's Lucky, Queen Gran's cat."

"Poor Lucky is stuck and she can't get down,"
says Alice. The broomstick stops near the cat.

The cat jumps on.

"Hold on, Lucky," says Alice. "You're safe now."
"Take us home please, broomstick," says Max.

They all fly back to the castle.

The broomstick whizzes through the window
and stops. Max, Alice and Lucky jump off.

"That was fun," says Max.

"Quick, put the broomstick back in the corner,"
says Alice. "I can hear someone coming."

Queen Gran comes in.

"There you are, my dears," she says. "I hope you have been good and not touched anything."

"Oh! There's Lucky."

"I have been looking for her everywhere,"
says Queen Gran. "I thought she was lost."

# "We've been a little naughty."

"But we did find Lucky," says Max. "It was the broomstick which found her," says Alice.

First published in 1996 by Usborne Publishing Ltd, 83-85 Saffron Hill, London EC1N 8RT, England. Copyright © Usborne Publishing Ltd.
The name Usborne and the device ⏚ are Trade Marks of Usborne Publishing Ltd. All rights reserved. No part of this publication may be reproduced, stored in a retrieval system, or transmitted in any form or by any means, electronic, mechanical, photocopy, recording or otherwise, without prior permission of the publisher. UE First published in America in August 1996. Printed in Italy.

# My First Sleepover

Charlotte Guillain

**www.raintreepublishers.co.uk**
Visit our website to find out
more information about
Raintree books.

**To order:**
☎ Phone 0845 6044371
📄 Fax +44 (0) 1865 312263
✉ Email myorders@raintreepublishers.co.uk

Customers from outside the UK please telephone +44 1865 312262

Raintree is an imprint of Capstone Global Library
Limited, a company incorporated in England and Wales
having its registered office at 7 Pilgrim Street, London,
EC4V 6LB – Registered company number: 6695582

Text © Capstone Global Library Limited 2011
First published in hardback in 2011
The moral rights of the proprietor have been asserted.

Edited by Dan Nunn, Rebecca Rissman, and Sian Smith
Designed by Joanna Hinton-Malivoire
Picture research by Elizabeth Alexander
Originated by Capstone Global Library Ltd
Printed and bound in China by Leo Paper
Products Ltd

ISBN 978 1 406 22051 3 (hardback)
15 14 13 12 11
10 9 8 7 6 5 4 3 2 1

**British Library Cataloguing in Publication Data**
Guillain, Charlotte.
    My first sleepover. – (Growing up)
    1. Sleepovers–Pictorial works–Juvenile literature.
    I. Title II. Series

793.2'1-dc22

**Acknowledgements**
We would like to thank the following for permission
to reproduce photographs: Alamy pp. 12 (© Image
Source), 14, 23 glossary homesick (© Catchlight Visual
Services); © Capstone Publishers Ltd pp. 5, 7, 11, 19, 23
glossary host (Karon Dubke); Corbis pp. 4, 23 glossary
relative (© JLP/Jose L. Pelaez), 9 (© Tony Metaxas/
Asia Images), 15 (© Christina Kennedy/fstop), 16 (©
Nicole Hill/Rubberball); Getty Images pp. 6 (Digital
Vision), 10 (Jupiterimages/FoodPix), 13 (Jupiterimages/
Brand X Pictures); Photolibrary pp. 8 (Corbis), 17 (SW
Productions/Brand X Pictures), 18 (Juice Images);
Shutterstock pp. 20 (© Vasiliy Koval), 21, 23 glossary
operation (© Monkey Business Images).

Front cover photograph of girls at a sleepover
reproduced with permission of Alamy (© Image
Source). Back cover photographs of a bathroom
reproduced with permission of © Capstone Publishers
(Karon Dubke), and camping reproduced with
permission of Shutterstock (© Vasiliy Koval).

Every effort has been made to contact copyright
holders of material reproduced in this book. Any
omissions will be rectified in subsequent printings if
notice is given to the publisher.

**Disclaimer**
All the Internet addresses (URLs) given in this book were
valid at the time of going to press. However, due to the
dynamic nature of the Internet, some addresses may have
changed or ceased to exist since publication. While the
author and publisher regret any inconvenience this may
cause readers, no responsibility for any such changes can
be accepted by either the author or the publisher.

# Contents

Some words are shown in bold, **like this**.
You can find them in the glossary on page 23.

# What is a sleepover?

A sleepover is when you stay overnight at someone else's house.

It could be at a friend's house or with **relatives**.

You may sleep at another house for one night, or sometimes for longer.

You may eat your evening meal and breakfast at a sleepover.

# Why do people have sleepovers?

Many people have sleepovers for fun.

Some people have a sleepover with friends to celebrate their birthdays.

You may go to a sleepover with friends or family if your parents are away.

Your parents might have to go into hospital or away for work or a trip.

# What do I need to take?

You need to take pyjamas, a toothbrush, and a change of clothes.

Sometimes you might also take your own sleeping bag to sleep in.

You might take something to remind you of home, such as a teddy bear or book.

You might like to take a photo of your family with you.

# What do I need to know?

It is a good idea to know what to expect on a sleepover.

Ask your **relative** or your friend's parents what will happen during your stay.

Find out where everything is and always ask if you need anything.

Make sure you know where the toilet and bathroom are.

# What might be different?

When you sleep over somewhere else, lots of things might be different.

You might try new or unusual food or eat meals at different times.

If you are staying with friends it might be exciting to stay up later than normal.

You might sleep on the floor or share a room for the first time.

# What should I do if I miss home?

You might miss your family and your own bedroom at home.

Tell your **relative** or friend and his or her parents if you feel **homesick**.

You might be able to phone your parents to make you feel better.

Try to keep busy and have fun doing something new.

# What makes sleepovers fun?

Sleepovers are fun because you do things in a different way to normal.

You might eat special food together.

It is fun to see your friends in a different situation, or spend time with a **relative**.

You might play games or watch a film together.

# What happens at the end?

You might feel tired in the morning if you stayed up late.

You will usually have breakfast before you go home.

Make sure you remember all your things and say thank you to your **host**.

You might like to give them a gift or a card to say thank you.

# When else might I stay away from home?

You might have to sleep away from home at other times.

You might go away on a school trip or go camping with cubs or the brownies.

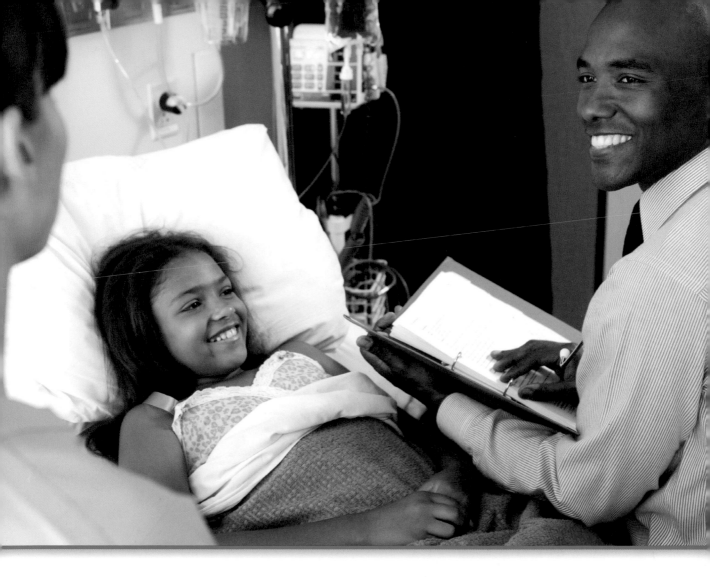

If you are ill or need an **operation,** you may have to stay in hospital for a while.

If you have been on a sleepover you won't feel so nervous if this happens.

# What to pack for a sleepover

- ✓ pyjamas
- ✓ a change of clothes
- ✓ toothbrush
- ✓ hairbrush
- ✓ towel
- ✓ sleeping bag
- ✓ teddy
- ✓ a gift

# Picture glossary

 **homesick** when someone misses their home and family

 **host** someone you go to stay with or visit who looks after you and makes sure that you have the things you need

 **operation** special treatment in hospital

 **relative** person in your family

# Find out more

## Books

*Harry and the Dinosaurs First Sleepover*, Ian Whybrow (Puffin, 2010)

*The Large Family: Sebastian's Sleepover*, Jill Murphy (Walker, 2009)

## Websites

You can sleepover with the dinosaurs at the Natural History Museum in London:
**http://www.nhm.ac.uk/visit-us/whats-on/nights-museum-events/dino-snores**

Or stay with daleks at the National Media Museum in Bradford:
**http://www.nationalmediamuseum.org.uk/sleepover/home.asp**

Your parents can help you find out about a sleepover in a museum near you.

## Index